HANS CHRISTIAN ANDERSEN

Thumbelina

Retold and illustrated by Brian Pinkney

GREENWILLOW BOOKS
An Imprint of HarperCollinsPublishers

Thumbelina
Copyright © 2003 by Brian Pinkney
All rights reserved. Printed in the United States of America.
www.harperchildrens.com

Colored inks on clay board were used to prepare the full-color art.
The text type is 17-point Cloister Old Style.

Library of Congress Cataloging-in-Publication Data
Pinkney, J. Brian.
Thumbelina / Hans Christian Andersen ; retold and illustrated by Brian Pinkney.
p. cm.
"Greenwillow Books."
Summary: A tiny girl no bigger than a thumb is stolen by a great ugly toad and subsequently has many
adventures and makes many animal friends, before finding the perfect mate in a warm and beautiful southern land.
ISBN 0-688-17476-0 (trade). ISBN 0-688-17477-9 (lib. bdg.)
[1. Fairy tales.] I. Andersen, H. C. (Hans Christian), 1805–1875. Tommelise. English. II. Title.
PZ8.P573 Th 2003 [E]—dc21 2002035320

First Edition 10 9 8 7 6 5 4 3 2 1

GREENWILLOW BOOKS

For Chloe

A woman who longed for a tiny child once asked an old lady for help. The old lady sold the woman a magic seed. Soon after the woman planted it, a beautiful, tightly curled blossom grew. Delighted, the woman kissed the petals, and the flower burst open. In its center sat a tiny girl.

"You're no bigger than my thumb," exclaimed the woman. "I will call you Thumbelina."

Each day Thumbelina played on the kitchen table, rowing on a little lake that was really a bowl of water decorated with flowers. Her boat was a tulip petal, her oars, two white horsehairs. She had a sweet voice, and she sang as she rowed. Each night she slept in a cradle made from a polished walnut shell.

One night, as Thumbelina slept, a toad crept in. "She will make a nice wife for my son," thought the toad. She snatched up Thumbelina in her cradle and rushed to the muddy river bank where she lived with her son. She left the sleeping girl on a water lily leaf in the middle of the stream while she helped her son prepare a room in the mud, where the couple would live.

The next morning Thumbelina wept to find herself in the middle of a stream, a prisoner of the toads.

Some fish overheard her and felt sorry for her. While the toads were carrying Thumbelina's cradle to the wedding chamber, the fish nibbled the stem that held the water lily leaf in place.

Soon the leaf and Thumbelina were floating free.

Thumbelina enjoyed the warmth of the sunshine and the songs of the birds.

When a butterfly landed on the leaf, she tied one end of her sash to the butterfly and the other end to the leaf. Pulled by the butterfly, the leaf gathered speed, taking Thumbelina far away from the toads.

A June bug flying by thought Thumbelina was the prettiest thing he'd ever seen, so he picked her up and put her on a leaf of a high tree. Thumbelina was frightened and very worried about the butterfly. She knew that it would starve if it couldn't free itself.

The June bug didn't care. He was too busy showing Thumbelina to his friends. But they thought she was ugly, so he set her on the ground and let her go.

All summer Thumbelina lived in the forest. She wove a hammock of grass and ate honey from flowers. She drank the dew that collected in leaves and listened to the songs of the birds. She was content.

When winter came, the flowers withered, and the birds flew away. Then the snows came.

Shivering with cold, Thumbelina wandered through the countryside, searching for food. She came upon a little house where a field mouse lived. When Thumbelina begged at the door for a grain of barley, the kind field mouse invited her inside.

"You may stay the winter," the field mouse told her. "But you must keep my house tidy and tell me a story every day, for I do like a good story."

Thumbelina was glad to agree.

The field mouse had a rich mole as a neighbor, and he came to call the next day. Before he arrived, the field mouse said to Thumbelina, "If you could get him for a husband, you would be comfortably off."

The mole was blind and did not share Thumbelina's love for the sun and for flowers. But when Thumbelina was asked to sing for him, he fell in love with her pretty voice. He was very cautious, so he said nothing about his feelings for her.

A week later, as Thumbelina strolled with the field mouse and the mole through one of the mole's underground passages, they came upon a dead bird.

The mole thrust his broad snout through the earth over the bird, and light shone down on its body. It was a swallow. The mole kicked it, saying, "What a misfortune to be born a bird!"

He closed the hole above the bird, and the mole and the field mouse walked on, but Thumbelina lingered to kiss the swallow's closed eyes.

That night Thumbelina wove a warm blanket out of hay. She took it to the dark passageway and covered the bird. For a moment she laid her head on his breast. To her amazement, she heard a thump. It was the sound a heart makes when it is beating! The swallow was not dead; he had been only numb with cold, and now he was reviving in the warmth.

Over the winter Thumbelina cared for the swallow secretly and grew very fond of him. By the time spring arrived, he was well and strong. Thumbelina reopened the hole in the roof of the passage so the swallow could fly away.

"Come with me, Thumbelina," he begged. But Thumbelina refused. She knew that the field mouse would be upset if she left.

Soon after the swallow had flown away, the field mouse told Thumbelina that the mole had asked for her hand in marriage. "You will have to make your wedding trousseau," the field mouse said.

And so Thumbelina had to spend the summer indoors, away from the sun, sewing wedding clothes for a marriage to someone she could not love.

When the trousseau was finished, the field mouse said, "Your wedding will be in four weeks' time." Thumbelina replied that she did not want to marry the mole. "Come, come," said the field mouse, "you are lucky to have him. "

On their wedding day the mole arrived to take Thumbelina to his home deep in the earth.

Before leaving, she stole outdoors to bid a sad farewell to the sun. She embraced a small red flower, saying, "Remember me to the dear swallow if you should see him!"

High above her, she heard a bird chirping.

The swallow had returned! How happy they were to see each other once more.

Upon learning that Thumbelina was about to marry the mole, the swallow said, "I am flying to the warm countries. Will you come with me? Dear little Thumbelina, do come."

"Yes, I'll come with you," said Thumbelina.

Thumbelina climbed on the bird's back and tied her sash to one of his strongest feathers. For the first part of the journey, she shivered in the cold air, but then she nestled among the bird's feathers and was comfortable.

At last they reached the warm countries, where lovely gardens bloomed.

"Choose a home for yourself in one of these flowers," the swallow said, setting Thumbelina on a leaf.

To Thumbelina's astonishment, each flower held a tiny person exactly her size. The king of the flower people, who wore a crown and had beautiful wings on his shoulders, bowed to her.

"How handsome he is!" whispered Thumbelina to the swallow.

The king gave her his crown and asked if she wanted to be his wife and the queen of the flower people. Thumbelina knew he was the right husband for her, and so she said, "Yes!"

The flower people brought wonderful gifts to Thumbelina.
The best gift of all was a pair of golden wings.

The wedding was held on a day of great joy, and Thumbelina
and the king of the flower people lived happily ever after.

The swallow liked to travel from country to country. On one of his journeys, the swallow built a nest under the window of a man who wrote stories. The swallow chirped the story of Thumbelina and her adventures to the man, who understood exactly what the swallow was telling him.

The man wrote down the whole story, and that is exactly what we have here!